Halloween Surprise

For Morgan —C. D.

To the goblins and ghosts by Halsey Road —R. W. A.

Text copyright © 2011 by Corinne Demas
Illustrations copyright © 2011 by R. W. Alley

First published in the United States of America in July 2011
by Walker Publishing Company, Inc., a division of Bloomsbury Publishing, Inc.
www.bloomsburykids.com

For information about permission to reproduce selections from this book, write to
Permissions, Walker BFYR, 175 Fifth Avenue, New York, New York 10010

Library of Congress Cataloging-in-Publication Data
Demas, Corinne.
Halloween surprise / by Corinne Demas ; illustrated by R. W. Alley. — 1st U.S. ed.
p.   cm.
Summary: Lily tries many different costumes before she creates the perfect one for surprising
her father on Halloween.
ISBN 978-0-8027-8612-8
[1. Costumes—Fiction. 2. Halloween—Fiction. 3. Cats—Fiction.] I. Alley, R. W. (Robert W.),
ill. II. Title.
PZ7.D39145Hal 2011   [E]—dc22   2010043434

The art for this book was created using pencil, watercolor, and gouache
Typeset in ITC Goudy Sans
Book design by Nicole Gastonguay

Printed in China by Toppan Leefung Printing, Ltd., Dongguan, Guangdong
10 9 8 7 6 5 4 3 2 1

All papers used by Bloomsbury Publishing, Inc., are natural, recyclable products
made from wood grown in well-managed forests. The manufacturing processes
conform to the environmental regulations of the country of origin.

Halloween Surprise

Corinne Demas

Illustrations by R. W. Alley

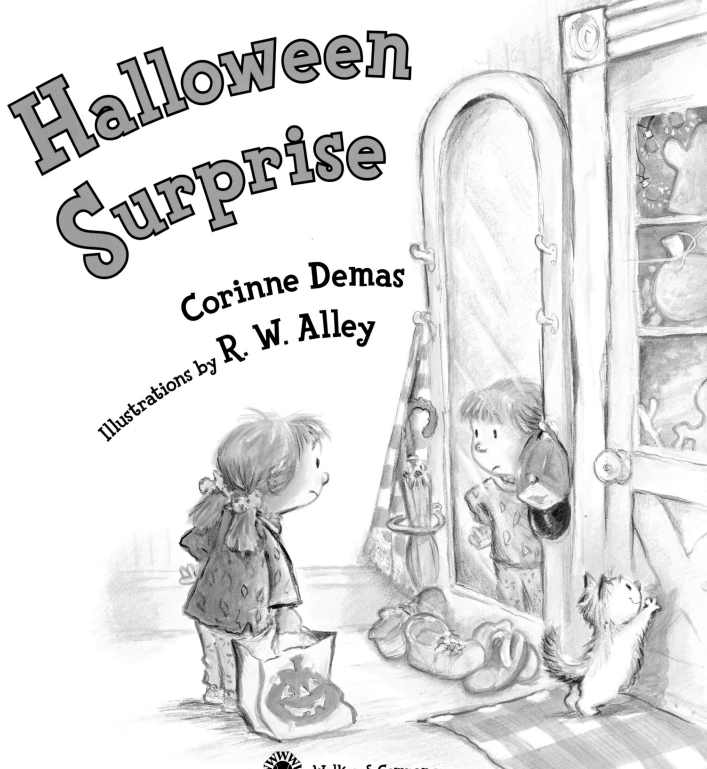

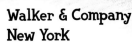

Walker & Company
New York

Halloween was almost here.
Lily wanted to make her own costume
to go trick-or-treating.

But she couldn't decide what she should be.

"What do you think?" she asked Fluff and Frisky.

How about a ghost?

Lily found an old white sheet
and cut holes so she could look out.
Boo!

Too scary!

How about a pirate?
Lily tied a bandanna around her head
and an eye patch over one eye.
She drew a black mustache on her face.

Too **MEAN**!

How about a pumpkin?
Lily cut out a cardboard pumpkin
and painted it all orange.
She tried to put it on.

Too **clumsy**!

How about a ballerina?
Lily put on her ballet slippers
and her pink tutu
from dance class.

Too flouncy!

How about a gypsy?
Lily put on a flowered shawl
and big hoop earrings.

Too **jangly!**

How about a princess?
Lily made a crown of gold paper.
She put on a long dress and lots
of pretend jewels.

Too *glittery!*

How about a robot?
Lily covered a big box with tinfoil.
She cut holes for her head and her arms
and her legs.

Too **bulky**!

Lily didn't have much time left.
What was she going to do?
She had to find a costume
for Halloween!

Lily looked at Fluff and Frisky.
Then she knew just what
she wanted to be.

Lily put on her white tights
and her hooded sweatshirt.
She cut two triangles out of paper
and taped them on the hood.
She found a rope and
attached it to her tights.
She painted her face.

"Let's go!" she called to Fluff and Frisky. They ran out the back door and around the side of the house . . .

. . . and rang the bell at the front door.

Daddy opened the door.
"Who's here?" he asked.

"Meow, meow!" said Lily. "That's
how kitties say Happy Halloween!"